Secrets I Know

Kallie George _and_ Paola Zakimi

schwartz & wade books · new york

I know lots of secrets. Like . . .

Secrets are for whispering.

Whispers hide in trees.

Trees make great umbrellas.

Umbrellas are the perfect boats.

Boats never listen.

But seashells hope you do.

Plus seashells make good saucers and tiny cups for tea.

You can sweeten tea with sunshine.

Sunshine marks the spot . . .

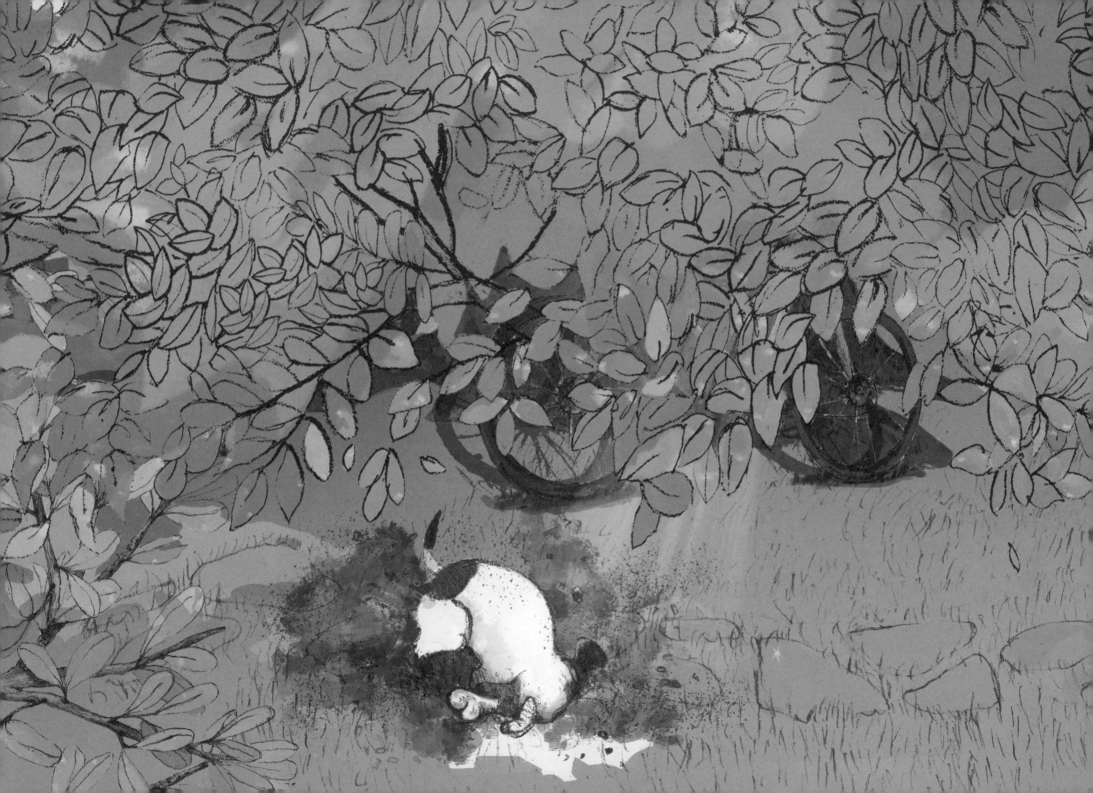

for finding buried treasure.

True treasure is a friend.

Together, friends are ladders.

Ladders lead to stars.

Stars keep your secrets.

They only tell the trees.

And trees make great umbrellas.

As you already know.

To Tiffany—true treasure really is a friend. —K.G.

To Juan and Sofi—you are my treasure. —P.Z.

Text copyright © 2017 by Kallie George • Jacket art and interior illustrations copyright © 2017 by Paola Zakimi • All rights reserved. Published in the United States by Schwartz & Wade Books, an imprint of Random House Children's Books, a division of Penguin Random House LLC, New York. • Schwartz & Wade Books and the colophon are trademarks of Penguin Random House LLC.

Visit us on the Web! randomhousekids.com • Educators and librarians, for a variety of teaching tools, visit us at RHTeachersLibrarians.com

Library of Congress Cataloging-in-Publication Data is available upon request.

ISBN 978-1-101-93893-5 (hc) — ISBN 978-1-101-93894-2 (lib. bdg.) — ISBN 978-1-101-93895-9 (ebook)

The text of this book is set in Belen. • The illustrations were rendered in pencil and colored digitally. • Book design by Rachael Cole

MANUFACTURED IN CHINA • 2 4 6 8 10 9 7 5 3 1 • First Edition